Kids love reading
Choose Your Own Adventure®!

"I loved the twists and turns of
the different endings."
Karianne Morehouse, age 12

"This is a flashlight-under-your-covers-book
to read at night. It's exciting, thrilling
and fun all at the same time."
Walker Curtis, age 11

"I like the places the author chose to put the
choices. It really makes it hard to put down
the book because it's like you're in the story."
Haley Behn, age 11

"It's really cool how you get to choose the end!
It made the book really fun to read."
Josh Farber, age 12

Watch for these titles coming up in the
Choose Your Own Adventure® series.

Ask your bookseller for books you have missed
or check online at Amazon.com.

CHOOSE YOUR OWN ADVENTURE® 17

THE BRILLIANT DR. WOGAN

BY R. A. MONTGOMERY

ILLUSTRATED BY
MARIANO TROD, CLAUDIO GRIGLIO, AND ANDRÉS ROSSI
COVER BY JOSE LUIS MARRON

CHOOSECO

A DIVISION OF CHOOSECO LLC
WAITSFIELD, VERMONT

The Brilliant Dr. Wogan ©1987 R. A. Montgomery,
Warren, Vermont. All Rights Reserved

Artwork, design, and revised text ©2005 Chooseco LLC,
Waitsfield, Vermont. All Rights Reserved

Illustrated by: M. Trod, C. Griglio, and A. Rossi
Cover illustrated by: Jose Luis Marron
Book design: Stacey Hood, Big Eyedea Visual Design
Chooseco dragon logos designed by: Suzanne Nugent

For information regarding permission, write to:

CHOOSECO
P.O. Box 46
Waitsfield, Vermont 05673
www.cyoa.com

ISBN 10 1-933390-17-4
ISBN 13 978-1-933390-17-8

Published simultaneously in the United States and Canada

Printed in Canada

0 9 8 7 6 5 4 3 2 1

For Anson and Ramsey

For Avery and Lila

and for Shannon

"There isn't a clue. Not a trace! Doctor Wogan, the brilliant Wogan, is gone."

The fat, stoop-shouldered official in the rumpled gray suit slams his pencil on the desk and sits down, not looking at anyone in the room. You glance around at the others. They are all silent.

Then, without warning, you hear:

"There is only one person who can find Diana Wogan and bring her back—if she's alive. We all know who I'm talking about. You, come up here." The man in the gray suit points at you.

You are the youngest scientist ever to be a member of the world-famous Delta Group, a research team dedicated to global peace. It's made up of people from both the small and the powerful countries. Doctor Wogan is the head of the group, and you are her right-hand assistant.

Turn to page 2.

2

The year is 2043, and rogue nations and terror groups have been threatening the use of nuclear weapons for more than forty years. Doctor Wogan has concentrated her research on a device that neutralizes radiation. "Just think," she has often said to you, "we can make nuclear weapons powerless if this device works."

"But Doctor Wogan," you replied recently, "in the wrong hands the radiation neutralizer could hold the world hostage. One group or country would be safe from attack, but the rest of the world wouldn't be."

"I know," she said. "That is why I must hurry to finish the device and give it to the entire world—so that everyone can have it."

Turn to page 8.

4

You have no opportunity to surrender. The next rocket explodes in the villa, ending all opportunity for action, now or in the future.

The End

The ferry for Bozcaada is an old boat, grimy with years of service. Barnacles and seaweed cling to its hull. It sloshes up and down in the gentle swell of the Aegean.

"One way or return?" asks the man selling tickets, in surprisingly good English.

"Return, I hope," you reply.

"As you wish," he murmurs, handing you your ticket.

The ferry does not depart for two hours. When at last it chugs away from Canakkale, you survey the other passengers. There are six of them.

Turn to page 18.

The square is filled with people. The man who bumped into you has been absorbed into the crowd of busy people on market day. He is nowhere to be seen.

"Well, here I go," you say. "The island can wait until another day."

"What's that?" an old woman asks, staring up at you out of a wrinkled face with milky blue eyes.

"Nothing! Nothing! Just talking to myself," you reply.

The woman stares at you for a few more moments and then she, too, is gone, swallowed up by the crowd of market-goers. The sun is fading in the late afternoon sky, and the air is growing cool. You pull your jacket tight, zip it up, and look for the Hotel Kristos.

Turn to page 9.

The day after that conversation, Doctor Wogan disappeared. She was probably kidnapped by someone or some group who wanted the plans for the device. But there is a chance that she has gone into hiding to work in safety.

Now you sit in Delta Group Conference Room B in a research complex just south of London. You don't protest when the official calls you forward. They would never take no for an answer, and besides, as Doctor Wogan's assistant you probably are most qualified to search for the genius. You rise slowly from your chair and walk toward the front of the room.

You place yourself at attention in front of the man in the gray suit.

"So," he says, "you know how important this job is. Without Diana Wogan, the work of the last eleven years, the hope of hundreds of millions of souls, and maybe even life as we know it on this planet, will be lost. L-O-S-T forever. It's sad that we humans have gotten to a point where so much depends on one person, but we have to BRING HER BACK ALIVE! Remember, there are many foreign agents after her and her plans. You won't be alone in your search for Doctor Wogan."

Turn to page 87.

The Hotel Kristos, an old stone building with thick oak doors, sits across from the church.

You take a deep breath and enter the hotel. It is dark and gloomy inside. You have a feeling this isn't an ordinary hotel.

A very small man dressed in a fancy scarlet uniform greets you with an unusually loud voice. "May I be of service?"

"Yes," you reply. "I want to sign up for Zabillh's show."

"Oh! So you want to see the Great Zabillh perform? I might have known. Well, follow me. I will take you to sign up. Be careful, the ceiling is low and the steps are uneven." He leads you toward the back of the dark lobby.

Turn to page 84.

10

You wish you could hide somewhere, but you are bathed in the harsh cabin light. Any sudden movement would be noticed. The Yenrotta moves slowly toward your table. He is staring right at you. His eyes have taken on a new look, an intense, burning gaze of recognition. At that moment you catch sight of the woman. She moves from behind a group of people, holding a weapon in her hand. The Yenrotta does not seem to see her. The next thing you know, the woman is surrounded by a group of passengers and disarmed. Shuddering, you await your fate. The Yenrotta speaks. "You are a troublesome and difficult person. But we do have a place for your kind, don't we?" The Yenrotta looks at the passengers. They nod. You realize the passengers aren't tourists. They're all working together.

"So off we go to a nice room at the Hotel Kristos. You will be comfortable there and we'll be able to keep an eye on you. You won't interfere with our plans, and we'll have a chance to get to know one another. We have a lot to talk about. Doctor Wogan and the radiation neutralizer, for example." He smiles a very unpleasant smile. You smile back. You might as well be pleasant. You have a feeling you and the Yenrotta will be spending a lot of time together.

The End

12

Doctor Wogan once told you that sound currents connected all things in the universe. Some sounds could be used for good; other sounds created evil. Now that you think back to those days in Doctor Wogan's labs and testing grounds, you recall the presence of soothing sound.

"Lead on," you hear yourself say in a distant voice, almost as if you are hearing a recording of your voice played in a tunnel.

You feel yourself drifting. You are relaxed, able to see clearly but unable to think quickly or normally. You are led away.

"I'm hypnotized," you say out loud. But your voice is a mere whisper.

Turn to page 95.

Desperately, you work the switch. Suddenly it slides to the on position.

The magnetic field reverser goes into immediate effect. There is a massive shuddering sound and a vibration so unsettling that you frantically try to return the switch to off. You don't succeed.

Turn to page 100.

14

"You can't scare me. Doctor Wogan is too powerful for you. You're bluffing. I'm leaving, and if you try to prevent me or harm me, you will pay. Look at this, and look at it carefully."

You remove the energy minimizer from your pocket and display it.

The small black object in your hand looks harmless, but the four people stare at it as if it were alive and could bite.

"I'm leaving now. I'm not kidding. Follow me and it's your funeral."

You mount the first rung of the stairs with your back turned to the three. You hear a sound. You stop. Slowly you turn. You finger the energy minimizer.

If you use it, who knows what will happen to the people in the room? Or to you, for that matter? But if you don't use it, how can you be sure you'll get up the stairs safely?

No one moves.

If you decide to switch on the energy minimizer, turn to page 27.

If you run up the spiral stairs, turn to page 42.

Carefully you examine the room, checking the walls, the floor, the bank of computer screens. The screens are blank, giving off only the greenish light.

You turn away from them, frustrated. In your frustration, you become careless.

By accident, you switch the action inhibitor off!

Within seconds you are in handcuffs and old-fashioned leg irons. The small man, carrying a flashlight, leads you to a windowless cell. You are infuriated by your own foolishness. You note with dismay a high watermark, indicating flooding near the ceiling. You may be doomed. Only time will tell.

The cell door clamps shut.

The End

A smartly dressed, middle-aged man steps into the room. "Come now, my good friend, you've had a bad time of it. Let's leave these dreary surroundings and see if we can have a pleasant little talk. Follow me."

You follow a tunnel from the subterranean chamber into a bright garden. The sun is at its zenith. You wonder how much time has passed. The digital read-out on your watch tells you it's noon.

"Doctor Wogan is with us," the man says. "However, she is, how should I say it? She is sick, or rather, incapacitated, at the moment. Perhaps you could help her."

"How?" you ask suspiciously.

"Well, interpret these papers of hers, and we'll release her to you. Simple. No risk," the man says. He hands you a sheaf of papers. You recognize at once what they are. They are Doctor Wogan's plans for the unfinished radiation neutralizer. They are, however, missing important bits of information.

"How did you get these?" you ask.

"We have our ways," he replies.

Turn to page 106.

The six passengers spread throughout the small cabin, each taking a seat near one of the windows. You have been traveling for several hours when one of them, a young woman dressed in a yellow rain slicker, motions to you with a nod of her head and a slight movement of her hand. She repeats the movement and looks aft, out toward the deck at the stern of the ferry. Then she gets up and leaves the cabin.

You are about to rise and follow her when a man, middle-aged and well-dressed in a suit and a tweed overcoat, attracts your attention by dropping a pen. He bends to pick it up, and while rising, gently shakes his head, looks at the figure of the woman who is now out on deck and mouths the word "No."

If you decide to ignore the man's warning and go out on deck to talk to the woman, turn to page 21.

If you decide to take the man's advice and not follow the woman, turn to page 92.

Out of the corner of your eye you become aware of movement inside the cabin. Two men are tiptoeing toward the door leading to the aft deck. You start to warn the woman that the men are coming, but suddenly you notice the glint of light on a metal object in the woman's hand.

Your heart is racing. Is the knife intended for the men? Or is it intended for you?

If you jump ship and swim for the island, turn to page 64.

If you warn the woman that the men are coming, turn to page 22.

Rising slowly to accommodate the swell of the waves, you ignore the frowning man and move outside the cabin. A moist and salty sea breeze greets you. It has already grown dark. The woman sitting next to the rail doesn't look at you. You take a position next to her. Both of you stare into the plume of white foam streaming behind the ferry.

Finally, she speaks.

"You are in great danger. I am your only friend on this boat. Beware of the others. Stay close to me and speak to no one. Doctor Wogan awaits." She still doesn't look at you. You have no opportunity to read what is in her eyes: truth or lies.

"Who are the others?" you ask.

"Your enemies! Yours and Doctor Wogan's and the world's. I can't say more. It is not important anyway."

You remember the note. It said you'd be contacted, but it did not say where or when. Is this woman your contact? Or is it the man who dropped the pen?

Turn to page 19.

22

"They're coming for us," you whisper loudly.

"Let them come," she replies. The cold tone of her voice frightens you.

The two men have reached the deck. They split up, one taking the port side and the other the starboard side, slowly moving in on the two of you.

"Okay, don't you move or you'll force me to do something we'll all regret," says the smaller of the two men. He holds a blunt-nosed revolver. The other man fingers a gleaming stiletto.

You back up, praying for a miracle. The woman laughs and points the shiny metal object at them.

Turn to page 36.

The story then tells of a dangerous period when the leader escapes to a remote island. As you read on, you begin to realize that the story is actually what has just been happening. It ends successfully because of the return and help of a trusted young associate. You gasp in amazement. There on the page is your own name! The date of the story is today! You drop the book, suddenly frightened. Somehow you have gotten your hands on a book from the future. You know that, aside from the radiation neutralizer, Doctor Wogan was working on experiments in time travel. You wonder if Doctor Wogan had a hand in this.

The van bumps along the road leading to your destiny. Whatever happens is clearly beyond your control.

The End

Swimming in the wake of the ferry is difficult, but you do your best. The water is very cold.

You've swum several yards when you see a rowboat bob over a wave. A man leans over the side.

"Get in before you freeze to death," he says in a heavily accented voice.

Grasping the gunwale, you climb aboard the small rowboat. You shiver fiercely.

"Here, drink this and put this coat on," he says.

The man hands you a cup of steaming hot soup from a thermos and gives you a wrinkled gray-green army overcoat.

The ferry has turned around. Its searchlights are scanning the water. Two rockets have gone up in arcs. Their light illuminates a large stretch of water, but the rowboat is outside the circle of light, at least for now.

"Here, shoot out the searchlights," the man says, handing you a rifle with a long-range night scope attached to its slender barrel. He is busy fitting an outboard motor to the stern of the rowboat.

"I didn't count on rockets, but they will burn out. Shoot out the searchlights. Those people mean to kill you."

Turn to page 26.

If you agree to follow the man's command, turn to page 48.

If you decide to ignore him, turn to page 40.

"I warned you," you shout, pointing the energy minimizer directly at the group. "Here goes."

The click of the on button reverberates in the room. You wait. At first nothing seems to happen. Then one of the people slowly raises an arm, drawing a pistol from a narrow black belt cinched around his waist. You realize the movements are all in slow motion.

It takes minutes for the person to raise the object, aim it, and fire.

"Zeeck . . ."

Turn to page 60.

Lunging forward, you stumble on the next step. Somewhere below you one of the people pulls out a weapon and fires. The first blast is wide of its mark. A bullet pulverizes a block of stone and ricochets off the metal handrail of the spiral staircase just below you.

"How did I ever get into this?" you ask yourself as you desperately climb the remaining steps.

Their weapon needs reloading, giving you precious time, but two of the attackers are close behind you on the stairs.

Turn to page 96.

30

You recall Doctor Wogan's often-repeated words: "Escape is central to all planning. You must always have an alternate route." Before taking one more step, you need to evaluate your options. The one thing the small man forgot to do was search you. Had he done so, he would have discovered three devices: all small, all electronic, all harmless-looking, but powerful tools nevertheless.

One of the devices is an action inhibitor, designed by Doctor Wogan to make an aggressor incapable of taking action without being harmed. Another device is an energy minimizer, a radical new device intended to slow down all molecular activity. Bullets float, punches seem cushioned in sponge, sound falls to pieces as if decaying. This device has never been used. The long-term effects are unknown. It is a spin-off from the radiation neutralizer.

The third device is something called a magnetic field reverser. Doctor Wogan had just developed it and you'd grabbed the model from her London lab before leaving. You aren't sure exactly what it does—better not experiment until you have to.

You slip your hand into your jacket pocket, trying to decide on the proper device and the best strategy. Should you use the action inhibitor or the energy minimizer?

Either way you have the magnetic field reverser as backup.

If you decide to use the action inhibitor, turn to page 39.

If you favor the energy minimizer, turn to page 14.

"I'll give them just enough information to tantalize them," you decide.

"What do you want to know?" you ask.

The voice comes from one corner of the room. "We have Doctor Wogan, but she went into a trance. She will not communicate with us. We fear she will die, and we are helpless to prevent this. If she dies, it will be a tragic loss to the world; we can't let it happen. We know you are close to Doctor Wogan and that you know about the radiation neutralizer. Help us."

"Well, what do you want?"

"Make her come out of the trance. We are a friendly private peace group. We only want to help. She thinks we're thieves. She said she'd die before dealing with us." The voice pauses. Then it continues.

"What proof does she need of our good intentions? We only wish to protect her from the real thieves. We got to her just to protect her—her and the world. There are greedy people out there who will do anything to get their hands on the only complete plans for the radiation neutralizer. If you know the final phases of the design, your life will be in danger. You'll be finished. But if you help us publicize the plans, then all the world will have the neutralizer. That's the only way to insure peace."

Turn to page 49.

"Doctor Wogan is my only . . ." you say, your voice trailing off until it's inaudible.

You slump against the wall and slip to the floor with a bone-jarring thud. Your eyes roll, you drool, and you speak garbled words. It is only half play-acting, since you hit your head hard when you fell. At least the sudden movement released you from the hypnotic trance.

Turn to page 50.

Once safely on the dock, you survey the crowd looking for a contact.

"Special bus to the castle. Great views, tourist special. Here's your ticket," says a man holding out a piece of paper. You look at the paper and see the name "Wogan" spelled out in big letters. The man nods and smiles. He gets in the bus and you follow.

The woman from the boat is already there! She's sitting next to a window. She motions to you to sit next to her. "Why didn't you come out on deck? I wanted to warn you about the opposition."

"I was scared, I guess. I didn't know who you were. I still don't."

"I'm Diana Wogan's daughter," she replies. "And we are in danger, in even greater danger than I first thought. The opposition thinks you are my mother's special courier. They will do anything to track you. It is a critical time. Mom has asked to see you. But if you will leave the bus, sacrificing yourself by serving as a decoy, my mother may escape, taking with her the possibility of a peaceful world. We have already been rescued from crooks and spies in Canakkale, thanks to you. The crooks were distracted by your arrival, and Mom was able to break away from them as they tried to follow you."

"And if I refuse to be a decoy?" you ask.

"Then stay aboard the bus, and we will do our best to lose them and help my mother escape."

If you decide to be a decoy, turn to page 41.

If you stay on the bus and go see Doctor Wogan, turn to page 52.

36

A fine mist shoots out and envelops the two men. They are immediately turned into laughing, giggling, friendly people. The short one flings his revolver over the side of the ferry as though it were an unwanted and loathsome thing. The man with the knife drops it into the water.

"Now you will both sit down on the deck and wait until dawn. Is that understood?" the woman says to the two of them.

"Yes. Sure. Why not?" they answer, almost in unison.

"What now?" you ask her.

"We wait until we dock. Then you either return to the mainland because—wisely—you fear for your life, or you throw in with us. We can't spend time with the faint-hearted. This is serious business, and personal safety and survival are of little importance. Doctor Wogan has spoken highly of you. And thanks to you, she has just managed to escape a band of thieves in Canakkale. They were distracted by your arrival and wanted to follow you."

Soon the ferry docks, and the landing ramp bumps into place. The two men are still under the effect of the gas. The woman looks at you, waiting for your decision.

If you decide to stay aboard the ferry and return to the mainland to work out a plan or to get help, turn to page 44.

If you decide to land and go to Doctor Wogan, turn to page 102.

The action inhibitor in your hand gives you a feeling of power. Its effects should buy you time to investigate this suspicious group. All you have to do is push the switch.

You push it.

"ZAM!"

Time freezes. The small man and the others are stop-action frozen. Their mouths are open as if speaking, arms and legs stuck in ridiculous poses, eyes open, unblinking and unseeing. Only you are free from this effect.

You have seen it work in the lab. Doctor Wogan said no harm would come to anyone under the power of the inhibitor.

You walk over to the man who seemed to be in charge and wave your hand in front of his face. No response. You speak to him.

"Not too scary now, are you?" you say.

No response.

"I guess it really works," you say. But do you trust Doctor Wogan's invention enough to search for her while her captors remain frozen?

If you decide to search for Doctor Wogan, turn to page 15.

If you decide to escape, turn to page 93.

40

The rifle rests on the seat next to you. You make no attempt to use it, despite his commands.

Once again you are in a situation beyond your control, a prisoner of circumstances, events, and maybe of this man who has pulled you out of the sea.

"What are you doing out here?" you ask him.

"Some say I was fishing," he answers, busying himself with an outboard motor.

"Fishing for what? At night, without running lights on your boat? Sounds odd to me," you reply.

"Well, look what I caught," he replies, smiling at you.

You don't like the gleam in his eyes.

Turn to page 55.

"I'll go" you say, summoning up all your courage. "If it gives Doctor Wogan time to escape, it's what I must do."

The young woman nods, and you get up from your seat. Your legs feel like they're weighted with lead, your feet seem to be unattached to your legs. Everything is dizzying and unreal. You move in a dreamlike state down the bus aisle, down two steps, and into the street outside, all the while waiting for a hail of bullets or worse.

Nothing happens. The bus starts up and moves off in a puff of diesel exhaust. You head for a taxi stand by a café across the small town square. People are milling about in the night, a mixture of tourists and locals. You try to look unconcerned, but your heart is beating so loudly that you fear the people on the street can hear it.

Turn to page 54.

The four people stay still. They must know about Doctor Wogan's inventions.

You mount the stairs, hoping their fear of your weapon will buy you some time. There's a movement behind you. You start to run. They are after you!

"Stop!" someone shouts. "Stop!"

You spin around and aim the energy minimizer at them, but to your horror it slips from your grasp and clatters down the spiral staircase, thudding to a stop on the stone floor of the chamber.

"Give up!" they yell.

You look up toward the top of the stairs, feeling for the other two devices in your pocket.

"Rely on instinct," you tell yourself. "That's what Doctor Wogan would do in a case like this."

If you run for it, turn to page 29.

If you use one of the other devices, turn to page 57.

The woman sounds like a fanatic, you think, and a fanatic is useless in helping Doctor Wogan.

For a few more moments you survey the scene: two giggling men sitting on the deck, a dedicated woman waiting for your answer, and a crowd of people leaving the ferry. A man on the dock attracts your attention. Tall, stocky, bearded and deadly serious, he is watching every person who leaves.

"He's looking for me. I know it. I can feel it in my bones," you say.

"Who? Where?" the woman asks quickly.

"Over there. That man," you reply.

"It's a Yenrotta!" the woman exclaims, turning her head and ducking behind you.

"A what?" you ask.

"A Yenrotta. A gun for hire. Don't ask questions. Just move into the main cabin and wait. Let's hope he didn't see us."

Turn to page 67.

You reach for the third device, but the delay has given your pursuers ample opportunity to catch up with you and surround you.

Your arms are pulled back, and handcuffs are snapped in place.

"Come with us. Be calm and we will not harm you. We want your help, not your life. You are so fearful. All people seem to be that way, even the great Doctor Wogan. Pity. If only you didn't fear the unknown so much. Oh, well. In time, perhaps." The voice is calm and soothing. You relax and allow yourself to be led away.

Turn to page 83.

You move toward the door. Odd, you think to yourself, that you had not noticed the dull green metal door. Perhaps you were too frightened to be aware of your surroundings.

Three steps, four, then two more and you reach out and push. The door yields. Soon you will make your getaway.

But when you enter the brightly lit room, you find that you are not alone. Before you are two figures. They stand with arms folded, feet wide apart, forming a barrier to someone behind them—Doctor Wogan. They look grim and dangerous.

At that precise moment Doctor Wogan gathers all her energy, all her great willpower, and creates a miniature explosion that terminates all beings in a radius of twelve feet. You, of course, are included.

The End

"Okay, but I'm not very good with weapons—never had much desire to use them," you say.

The man pauses for a moment, giving the engine-mounting brackets one last twist. He pushes the outboard down so that the small propeller is in the sea. Before pulling the starter cord he says quietly, "Aim high. Squeeze the trigger—don't pull it. Fire again if you don't succeed."

"But there are people aboard the ferry! What if I hit them?" you cry, scared and worried.

"Too bad for them! There are victims everywhere in the world. That is just bad luck. Now, fire!"

You shake your head and put the gun down on the seat next to you. "No, I can't do it. I don't want to kill anyone. It's wrong," you say.

"Suit yourself. It's your life. I'll do it."

He grabs the rifle, aims, and squeezes the trigger. There is a popping sound, a small flash, and then the main searchlight on the ferry winks out. The man fires again. The ferry's other light goes out. Now only the bright white flares remain, and they are about to fall into the sea.

The motor launch from the ferry is heading for you.

Turn to page 70.

You don't believe the man. "This is no peace group," you say to yourself, "They're crooks."

Doctor Wogan once told you that in the event of serious trouble, you were to do your best to return to her private laboratory and either destroy the plans or have the completed ones published yourself. Her greatest fear was that the plans would fall into the wrong hands.

"Why not publish them now?" you had asked.

"They're not finished," she had replied sadly.

At the very least, you were never to give any help to Doctor Wogan if she were a prisoner. She preferred death to giving up the plans. But are you willing to have Doctor Wogan's death on your hands?

If you decide to try to get Doctor Wogan out of her trance and save her life anyway, turn to page 76.

If you decide to try to escape, turn to page 53.

50

The room spins, the light intensifies, your head begins to clear, but you pretend to remain only semi-conscious. You open your eyes, millimeter by millimeter, surveying the room through your eyelashes.

It's empty! You sit up.

"They're gone," you sigh in relief. You feel your legs and arms, your head, your hands. Everything seems all right. You stagger to your feet and begin an investigation of the surrounding area.

A door in the stone wall attracts your attention. To your surprise, it opens.

Turn to page 16.

"I'm going with you, Doctor Wogan," you say.

"Okay. Our escape will be dangerous and exhausting. I'll be glad to have you along, my dear friend."

You nod your agreement.

Preparations are made in quiet.

Finally, you and Doctor Wogan are in a boat. You cast off and bid farewell to your silent companions on shore: several men and the bus driver. They will act as decoys for the enemy. Doctor Wogan's daughter has already left for a safe house inland. An hour later, as you sail quietly through the heaving sea, you see a brilliant flash of light. You think that it is probably an explosion at the villa. You are concerned about those left behind, but what you must concentrate on is what's ahead.

At dawn you reach land. You abandon the boat and head inland.

Turn to page 68.

52

"Hey, I'm no sitting duck for anyone!" you exclaim. "I'm here to help, but that's crazy. It sounds like suicide. Besides, you said Doctor Wogan wanted to see me."

"As you wish," she replies.

The bus moves off, and minutes later it is traveling along a narrow bumpy road, perilously close to a cliff that falls straight to the ocean below. The bus driver has turned out the lights and is driving very fast. You hope he knows what he's doing.

Turn to page 56.

"This won't be easy," you say to the man. "Doctor Wogan is strong, perhaps the strongest-willed person I have ever met. If she doesn't want to give information to you, nothing will get her out of the trance. But I will try. Perhaps she has misjudged you and your intentions."

The man nods his head vigorously in agreement with your notion that Doctor Wogan may have misunderstood. "Yes, yes. Very good. We intend no harm," he says earnestly. "We are anxious for the world to receive Doctor Wogan's great plans. That is all. We are for peace only. Doctor Wogan is in that room," he says, pointing. "Behind that green door."

"I must be alone with her," you say. The man nods agreement, stands back, and lets you pass.

You don't like the looks of that man. *He probably spells peace G-R-E-E-D,* you think.

Turn to page 47.

"Taxi!" you say in what you hope is a normal tone.

A cab pulls up. Its driver leans out the window.

"Yes, my friend," he says, "and where do you wish to go?"

You think for a moment. "Around the island. Yes, that's it, around the island. Just a little night-time tour," you reply.

"But of course, my pleasure."

Turn to page 79.

The man leans over, picks up the rifle, aims at the ferry boat, and just as he is about to fire, you lunge at him, knocking him and the gun into the sea.

"Hey! Help, I . . ." he yells in a splutter of rage and surprise. "I can't swim!" His head is pulled under the swell, then reappears. He tries desperately to cling to the boat. The motor launch from the ferry is nearing. The fear in his eyes fills you with sympathy.

You'd pass him a life preserver, but you remember how cold the water is—he might freeze before he is picked up. On the other hand, if you bring him aboard, he might attack you. You know you can't let him drown.

If you decide to pull him aboard,
turn to page 66.

If you decide to give him the only life preserver
and try to escape using the outboard,
turn to page 63.

56

Thirty minutes later, the bus slides to a stop in the gravel courtyard of a gray stone villa perched at the edge of the sea. You see several figures move from the shadows of a high wall. They approach the bus cautiously.

"Is the person here?" one asks carefully.

"Yes," the driver replies.

You realize that they are talking about you.

"Doctor Wogan wants to leave immediately. I think it is dangerous just now. She will be exposed if she leaves. We can protect her here," says one of the men.

"Well, you know Doctor Wogan. She does what she wants," the driver says. "How about this one? What does Doctor Wogan want this person for?" They are speaking about you again.

"Doctor Wogan says this is the one who can help her with the plans," the first man replies.

Turn to page 73.

You reach for the action inhibitor, and grab the magnetic field reverser instead. Oh well, you think—there's a first for everything.

But the on-off button sticks! It won't move!

Was this Doctor Wogan's way of protecting you? What if the magnetic field reverser is too powerful to be used?

If you decide to try the last remaining device, turn to page 45.

If you force the on-off switch, turn to page 13.

"We can't stay here and be targets," you shout from the floor. "Is there a hidden way out?"

"Quick. The basement stairs lead to a tunnel exit in the water," says one of the men. "Follow me."

Moments later you all stand knee-deep in water, wrestling with an old fishing boat, trying desperately to free it from its mooring. Behind you, a second shell explodes.

"I thought we were going to fight," you say.

"Against those weapons?" comes the answer.

Finally the boat is freed. The others climb in.

"Coming?" they ask you.

"No. I'll stay and see if I can buy you and Doctor Wogan more time."

They leave, only to be intercepted by a launch a mile offshore.

You stay, waiting for the worst.

The End

"This might be my last chance," you say to yourself, struggling as hard as you can against your captors. You kick, butt with your head and swing your hands and arms in a wide arc, hoping to strike anyone in range.

"Calm down! No one is going to hurt you," commands a firm and familiar voice. "We had to make it look realistic, grabbing you the way we did, but we're not your enemy."

"Tell me another," you reply.

One of the men steps forward and strips off a plastic mask. It's not a man at all.

"Doctor Wogan!" you shout, amazed and happy at finding your mentor.

"Correct. Now let's get out of here. By the way, this is my daughter," she says, motioning to the young woman from the boat.

The End

The bullet burbles through the air, tumbling and wavering. It falls to the ground and bounces like rubber. Then it melts into a million shimmering pieces, like bits of confetti, that spill over the stone floor.

"Try again," you say, taunting the group.

"Zleep!"

Once again, a bullet is emitted from the muzzle of the weapon. This time it decays in mid-flight and drops harmlessly to the floor!

You stare at the object in your hand and begin to laugh. "Good old Doctor Wogan," you say. "She's done it again!"

At that moment the four people make a dash for you. The effects of the energy minimizer must be wearing off!

Turn to page 98.

"Take this. Good luck," you say, tossing the yellow canvas life jacket to the man floundering in the water.

"I'll drown," he wails, kicking and spluttering.

"Use the life jacket. Stay calm. Wait for your friends," you tell him.

"They're not my friends!" he screams.

The motor starts. You push him off the side of the boat, making sure he is in the life jacket, and head toward the darkened shoreline of the island.

Turn to page 103.

64

SPLASH!

The shock of the cold water almost knocks you out. You jumped far enough out to escape the terrible suction of the ferry's propellers, but now you are fighting to regain the surface in a froth of bubbles. The wake pummels you. At long last you reach the surface, gasping for breath.

"Where is it?" you say out loud, getting a mouthful of salt water for your effort. "Where is Bozcaada?"

The ferry plows on, and you see three people on the stern. You can't tell whether they are pointing at you, struggling with the woman, or trying to help you. A second later there's a splash off the stern.

"It's probably a life preserver," you say to yourself. "I hope it's not one of them, dead or alive."

Turn to page 24.

The van is moving on a bumpy road. You wait until things have been quiet for a while. Then, summoning all your strength and energy, you kick out of the burlap bag with an enormous lurching thrust. Your hands fly up, ready to strike anyone.

"YEOW!" you shout.

There is no one with you in the back of the van. You are alone! The van looks completely empty. Then you notice something peculiar: on the floor of the van lies a book. A bookmark of red leather is stuck in it. There is no title on the cover or the spine. As you are examining the book, the rear door swings open as the van hits a bump.

If you want to open the book, turn to page 81.

If you forget the book and prepare to jump, turn to page 112.

66

"Hold on. I'll get you aboard," you say.

Leaning over as far as possible, you grab the man by the collar of his coat and heave him upward. He splutters and splashes, flapping on the gunwale like a fish. The rifle is gone.

The man flops into the boat, soaked, exhausted, but perhaps still dangerous.

You move to the stern, grasping one of the oars as a weapon in case he launches an attack, and manage to start the outboard. Relying on instinct, you head toward the darkened outline of the island. The searchlights from the ferry crisscross the water. You hear the powerful roar of the launch across the waves.

Soon you turn into a cove on the shoreline. The cove is protected by a series of large rocks that are bathed in the swell of the waves. A launch is patrolling back and forth. Your boat comes to rest with a crunch on the pebbly, sandy beach.

"Don't say a thing," you whisper to your prisoner.

He nods to affirm the command.

Turn to page 105.

The stream of people getting off the ferry merges with those now getting on for the return trip to the mainland. It is quite easy to lose oneself in the crowd. Surveying the dock, you realize to your dismay that the man identified as a Yenrotta is no longer to be seen! Where is he? you wonder. Maybe he's aboard the ferry. You turn to warn the woman, but she's gone!

Turn to page 71.

You've only taken a few steps when a voice stops you.

"Halt, who goes?" asks the firm voice.

"The light of the world," Doctor Wogan replies.

"Welcome," is the response.

A man dressed in the rough clothes of a herdsman leads you to two horses tethered to a low-lying tree. A map, a compass, and a wish for good luck are given to you. Then you are off. There is no time to rest; it is a long way to the border, and the people who want Doctor Wogan are relentless. The trip will hold many dangers.

"Who was that man?" you ask Doctor Wogan, wondering how extensive her network is.

"A cousin. I'm related to many in these parts," she says.

Turn to page 80.

"Get down," the man in the boat says. "Don't provide them with a target."

"Who are they?" you ask.

"Crooks, thieves, spies. Who cares? They want you and Doctor Wogan. They have been following you from London just as we have."

You look at the man in surprise, but he just pulls the starter cord, and the outboard coughs and then sputters into a steady but not very powerful chugging. The boat heads into the wind and rides the waves.

There is water in the bottom of the boat, mixed with oil and gas from years of use. You huddle down in the slime, hands resting on a thwart.

"Where are we going?" you ask.

"You'll see. Leave it to me," is the man's reply.

The launch is gaining. Off to the port side you see one more flare arch across the sky. Its a dud and falls harmlessly to the sea.

Turn to page 99.

You hear three blasts on the horn, the ramp goes up, the powerful engines reverse, and the ferry moves away from the dock. You try to make yourself as small as possible, huddling among the crowd of people occupying the table where you sit in the passenger cafeteria. The smell of licorice and of strong black coffee permeates the room.

The Yenrotta suddenly appears in the cafeteria. He surveys the crowd carefully, searching, evaluating, searching again.

Turn to page 10.

The driver motions for you to get off the bus. You do, and then you are told to follow the men into the villa. Doctor Wogan's daughter goes with you. Dimmed flashlights are used to guide you through long hallways until you reach a medium-sized room.

"Doctor Wogan!" you say in a loud, surprised voice.

"Welcome, young friend. Time is of the essence. I must move fast," she replies.

"Why?" you ask. "Isn't the island safe?"

"No! We have just arrived and already they know where we are. The key to world peace is the radiation neutralizer. We must finish it and give the plans to the world. I went into hiding to try to finish it on my own, but I've had enemy agents on my trail since the beginning. I've got to leave Bozcaada. I've escaped from Canakkale, where I was held prisoner, and the agents are still after me."

"How will you go?" you ask.

"Boat to the mainland, in disguise by horse to the border, then train, and finally plane," Doctor Wogan replies.

"But where to?" you ask.

Turn to page 74.

"Back to England," she responds. "I'm almost finished with the plans."

"Doctor Wogan, I want to come with you! You might need me. I'm your best protector! You always said I had a sixth sense about things—especially danger."

"Yes, you could help me escape, but perhaps I should give you my latest work. Then, if I'm captured, you can finish the plans. I have faith in you. I leave it up to you, my friend. You can stay here and finish the plans, if necessary, or you can come with me.

If you want to go with Doctor Wogan, turn to page 51.

If you stay behind with the latest plans for the radiation neutralizer, go on to the next page.

Loneliness settles over you as you watch Doctor Wogan leave for the mainland in her small boat. The people standing around you are silent and saddened also. That's always the way it is with Doctor Wogan, you think. People love her and become dedicated to her. "Well, let's get to it," you announce. "It's time to prepare for the worst. Inside now."

You surprise even yourself at how quickly you take command of the situation. Leadership is natural to you, but at your age, it still is surprising that these people—the bus driver, Doctor Wogan's daughter, and the men at the villa—all respond to you without questioning your authority.

Inside the villa, you ask them to gather around a table to plan for defense against attack and for your escape.

Turn to page 89.

"Lead me to her," you say, trying to sound brave and confident. Your legs feel like putty, your stomach like a cement mixer, and your heart like a jackhammer. "Lead me to her."

Doctor Wogan is sitting in a chair in the next room. Her face is composed. She looks younger and happier than at any other time you've seen her. Her color is good.

"She looks fine to me," you say.

"Yes, but she has been this way for six weeks without food or water. She will die if she doesn't come out of the trance."

"She's in hibernation," you respond.

"Evidently. But her pulse rate is almost nonexistent. There's a limit to how long even famous yogis who practice this strange art can go on. I'm afraid of brain death."

Turn to page 91.

You climb inside and the cab pulls away from the curb—but not before two people wearing fishermen's clothing climb in, one in front, the other in back next to you. They smell of garlic and tobacco.

"Let's get going," says the man sitting next to you. "We've got our catch for the day. This one is a fine specimen, no?"

The taxi accelerates and night swallows you in the folded hills of Bozcaada. You have been kidnapped, and you will be held for ransom. The ransom is probably Doctor Wogan and her plans. Your chances are not good, but at least there's a chance you'll go down in history as a hero.

The End

Toward noon, you see a band of men on horses moving in your direction. You look to Doctor Wogan to see if these men could be more of her "relatives." By the look on Doctor Wogan's face, you know she wasn't expecting to see anyone.

If you decide to run for it, turn to page 104.

If you want to hide, turn to page 111.

Curiosity has always been one of your strong points, or so you have thought. The book that was placed or dropped next to the burlap bag is too tempting to ignore. It must have been put there for a reason. You open it to the pages where the book-mark rests.

Reading quickly, you guess that it is a translation of an old folk tale. It tells of a powerful leader who overcomes evil for the good of the people. This leader is constantly being chased, attacked, and harassed by gangs and groups of the evil and corrupt. The story sounds surprisingly familiar. You wonder how the book got here and what it means.

Turn to page 23.

You don't trust your companion one bit, so you're not going to let him out of your sight.

You head up a steep slope, stumbling on the rocks in the dark. As you make your way, he chatters incessantly.

"You really should've trusted me. I really am one of Doctor Wogan's assistants. She's told me all about the radiation neutralizer. It's fascinating, especially the unfinished parts."

His constant talking irritates you. It's difficult to formulate a plan with all this talk.

"So," continues the man, "Doctor Wogan told me that you knew the rest of the plans. She intended to tell me but we had no time."

You know that you were right not to trust this man, but now what are you going to do? You are no closer to finding or helping Doctor Wogan than you were when you left Canakkale on the ferry. There's only one thing you can do—separate from this man and start over again.

You set the man loose and make your way back to the ferry. The poster with Doctor Wogan's photo had directed you to the Hotel Kristos. After a quick, but exhausting return trip, you make it to the hotel in time for the Zabillh's show.

Turn to page 9.

Days later, you and Doctor Wogan wake up in a wildflower field high in the mountains. You vaguely remember lengthy interviews with your captors. The interviews were like friendly conversations. No force, no persuasion, only talk. Then there was a murky period, and now you are awake, alive, and in this pasture. You turn to the brilliant doctor. "Doctor Wogan?" you say.

She looks at you, puzzled. Then she says slowly, "I feel as if I'm waking from a bad dream. There are enormous gaps in what I can remember. They've tampered with my memory . . . and they've got the radiation neutralizer."

The End

Silently, a stone wall slides open on gleaming metal hinges, revealing a stainless steel spiral staircase. A greenish light comes from below, a cool current of air blows up the steps. You hesitate.

"Go ahead. Have no fear," says the small man. This time his voice is no more than a faint whisper.

It takes several minutes to descend the stairs. At last you reach the source of the green light. It comes from a cavelike room of solid rock. The light is generated by a bank of computer monitors. Three people huddle over the central screen. They straighten up at the sound of your approach.

Turn to page 90.

You believe this intense woman. There is even a distinct resemblance to Doctor Wogan. "Will you help?" she asks again.

You nod.

"Good," she replies. "Follow me. My mother has just arrived after escaping from a band of thieves in Canakkale. She was able to break away from them when the thieves were distracted by your arrival and began to follow your movements. Here, put on these clothes. It is three hours by foot to her hiding place. From a distance, we will pass for farmers."

You head off to meet Doctor Wogan and once again to be her close aide and assistant. With luck, the radiation neutralizer will be finished, and the world will finally have a defense against nuclear weapons.

The End

Your only clue to Doctor Wogan's whereabouts is that she had an island retreat in the Aegean Sea off the coast of Turkey. The name of the island is Bozcaada. The closest city on the mainland is Canakkale.

Three days later, you have reached Canakkale. A poster on the stone wall of a church in a square immediately catches your attention. There's a picture of a woman on the poster.

"It's Doctor Wogan! It's her!" you shout. Slowly you translate the poster with the aid of a Turkish phrase book. It says:

SPECIAL APPEARANCE OF ZABILLH
THE GREAT FORTUNE TELLER
MARCH 9, 10:30 PM
PLACE TO BE ANNOUNCED
SIGN UP NOW AT HOTEL KRISTOS

It is now 4:30 PM

Is the poster a sign meant especially for your eyes? Is the sign from Doctor Wogan—or from those against Doctor Wogan?

Turn to page 94.

"So, who are they, what can we do, who will do what?" you ask, looking at each face carefully.

Doctor Wogan's daughter answers. "They are a group of international criminals who deal in drugs, slavery, espionage, and anything else that will turn a profit. They operate like a business. They are efficient, brutal, and dedicated—dedicated to money. They want those plans."

"So what do we do?" you ask again.

"We could join them," the bus driver answers, laughing in a loud voice.

At that moment a high, piercing whine invades the room.

"Attack!" yells one of the villa guards.

You all dive for the floor just as a rocket explodes against the side of the villa. You know the villa can't be defended against attack by heavy arms, and your only chance of survival is to surrender and outsmart the enemy. On the other hand, the longer you fight, the more time Doctor Wogan has to get away.

If you think you should surrender, turn to page 4.

If you want to take action, turn to page 58.

90

A murmuring sound, not quite music, fills the room.

"That's Doctor Wogan's sound," you think, startled. Many times when you were Doctor Wogan's assistant, she would close her eyes, sit upright with arms and legs crossed, and emit a sound just like the one you are hearing. It is a sound made during meditation, the sound *om* repeated over and over again.

Is Doctor Wogan making the sound? If so, where is she? Is she working here? It's just as likely she's being held captive.

"Here is one who is brave enough to meet Zabillh. Will this one do?" the dwarf asks.

"Yes. Perfectly," replies the figure in the center with a knowing grin. "Prepare our visitor."

"Will you come now?" you are asked.

If you decide to go with them (and investigate the sounds on the way), turn to page 12.

If you try to escape (because you think this may be a setup), turn to page 30.

You approach Doctor Wogan, glad to see her but worried that you might be making a mistake by trying to save her. Obviously Doctor Wogan is frightened by these people and does not trust them. That explains the trance, you think.

Doctor Wogan slowly moves her head. A look of wonder and sadness fills her eyes.

As you lean over her, she slides to the floor. You check her pulse. There is none. Doctor Wogan is gone. She takes her plans with her, except for what you know. Doctor Wogan has left you the enormous responsibility of being the sole caretaker of the secret of the radiation neutralizer. You look for a way out. There is none.

The End

It is too dangerous to trust anyone yet. That woman could be an enemy, and she could easily push you into the water.

"Maybe I'll be contacted on the island," you say to yourself.

The ferry sways in the waves, and you begin to experience a mixture of seasickness and fear.

The woman remains on the deck. She turns occasionally to stare at you, but she does not move, nor does anyone else in the cabin. It is unnaturally quiet. The only sound is the pumping beat of the ferry engine.

You realize you're going to be sick, and desperately look for a door to the deck that does not lead to the stern. You get to your feet, and, to your surprise, so does everyone else in the cabin. Then you notice that the ferry is at the dock. There is a thud as it gently bumps against the piers. With great relief, you forget your seasickness and head for the landing ramp with the other passengers.

Turn to page 35.

"I've got to get out of here. I can't do much for Doctor Wogan until I get help."

You head for the spiral staircase and climb as quickly as you can. As you search frantically for the device that activates the stone wall, you wonder how long the effects of the action inhibitor last. Suddenly the wall slides open, and with great speed you enter the lobby of the hotel.

There, to your surprise, stands the brilliant Doctor Wogan. She's smiling.

"Well done, my young friend. Well done. Come with me. We have work to do. I knew I could count on you," she says.

"But I didn't do anything," you reply.

"Yes, you did. You inhibited their movements, thus releasing me from their power. They are strong, but we are stronger! Now, to complete escape. Quickly! Let's be off! No time to waste. The world awaits our discovery."

The End

As you stare at the poster, a faint wind carrying the smell of rosemary and oregano sifts through the air. A middle-aged man slips on a cobblestone and bumps into you.

"Pardon me," he murmurs, while slipping a piece of paper into your hand. He moves off. The paper says: "Take the next ferry to the island of Bozcaada. You will be contacted. Beware of the lighted steps. Doctor Wogan lives, but there is great danger."

What now? you wonder. Should you trust this stranger?

If you decide to stay for the meeting with Zabillh, turn to page 7.

If you decide to go to Bozcaada by ferry, turn to page 5.

The murmuring increases in intensity until it reverberates so intensely you feel as though you were in a huge pinball machine, being bounced back and forth by the murmuring sound waves.

"I . . . MUS . . T . . . WA . . KE . . . U . . P . . . "

Immobilizing blackness slips into your shoes and floods upward through your body, until only your head is above it.

"Tell us what you know of Doctor Wogan!"

"What?" you manage to gasp.

"You know what!" the voice replies. "We have spies who tracked you from the moment you left Delta Group offices in London. We want information. Now tell us all you know."

Maybe if you tell them a little, they'll let down their guard and you can find a way to escape. On the other hand, if you pretend to pass out, you could buy some time while telling them nothing.

If you pretend to pass out, turn to page 32.

If you decide to tell what you know, turn to page 31.

96

"I made it!" you yell in triumph as you reach the last step. Another shot rings out, but it bounces off the top step, not touching you.

You dash for the door, knocking over a large man and his equally large wife who have just entered the hotel lobby.

"Sorry about that," you shout as you streak out into the square. You lose yourself in a crowd of people who are gathered around a series of open air stalls selling cheeses and meats, wine, sweaters, dried fruits, and old books.

You are safe now. To your amazement, you turn and see Doctor Wogan standing next to you.

"Doctor Wogan! You're safe!" you exclaim.

"Thanks to you, I escaped in the confusion down there, but we must get to my island. Hurry. There isn't much time."

The End

98

You push the force dial on the energy from +2 to +8.

A familiar voice fills the chamber.

"No! No! It's too much!" the voice yells.

It's Doctor Wogan!

"Okay, Doctor Wogan," you say. Frantically you reduce the effect of the energy minimizer by returning the dial to +2, and then beyond to +1.

Turn to page 108.

The launch accelerates and catches up with you. "What now?" you demand.

"Nothing. Nothing for you," replies the man.

The launch is traveling alongside you, and you recognize the well-dressed man in the tweed overcoat. He signals with a wave of his hand and the engine of the rowboat is cut.

"This is as far as I go," says the man in the rowboat. "You're all theirs now. The people I work for aren't paying me enough for me to risk my own life. These folks can have you."

You are transferred roughly to the launch, which speeds off toward a rocky coast-line at the southern end of the island. Soon you reach land.

In the dark you see a long stone staircase. Each step is lighted by a small bulb. At the top of the steps you dimly make out a group of buildings. No light shines in them.

"You will be staying here for quite some time," says the man in the tweed overcoat. "You have information we want, and we will get it." He retreats down the lighted steps, leaving you in the hands of two burly men.

The End

100

From the outer edge of the Milky Way Galaxy, a lone technician in an Orbital Heavens Observatory notes the sudden disappearance of a minor planet from the scanning screen.

The End

102

"I'm game, let's go," you say to the woman.

Once on the dock you follow her, but within minutes you are surrounded by a group of workers in blue coveralls. They grab you, thrust you in a large wheelbarrow, cover you with burlap sacks and hurriedly move off the dock.

You hear a shout, a woman's voice. Then all is quiet. You choke on the gag in your mouth and struggle against crude handcuffs of twisted wire. As soon as you free your hands you remove the gag. Just as you start to break out of the burlap bag, you are grabbed roughly and lifted into a van or truck.

If you fight and lose, your captors will re-tie your hands. But if you wait, who knows where they'll take you in the van.

If you decide to put up a fight, turn to page 59.

If you wait to see what happens, turn to page 65.

Dawn finds you safely hidden in an isolated farm shed on a hill above a small town. You can see the ferry at its dock. People are hurrying to get aboard for its morning run to the mainland. It seems so calm and tranquil from your vantage point on the hillside. The people and the boat are toylike. You feel as though you have awakened from a bad dream. Getting up, you stretch your arms to the sky. Suddenly, you feel a pistol barrel in the small of your back.

"Keep those hands up. Don't move or I'll be forced to shoot."

Turn to page 107.

104

"Doctor Wogan, get going, it's our only chance!" you yell, striking your horse with the crop and kicking hard. You don't get far. You are surrounded, captured, interrogated, and imprisoned, along with Doctor Wogan.

"My young friend, it seems like disaster, but wait, just wait," Doctor Wogan says to you as you sit together in the stone cell of your prison. "Patience. The plans they took from me are not only incomplete but deliberately misleading. Only you and I know how to interpret them properly. We'll never talk, will we?"

The End

The launch cruises by, penetrating the darkness with a powerful but narrow searchlight beam. There are so many rocks and inlets that you may remain undetected. Suddenly you realize the men must think you're still in the boat. You decide to start the motor, fix the steering, and push the boat out to sea.

You do this, and the rowboat heads out, bumping across waves. You watch it gain the open water.

"Soon they'll pick it up. We don't have much time. Let's go," you say to your companion.

Turn to page 82.

106

The man lights a cigarette and blows smoke rings slowly in your direction.

"Help us with these papers. We must have the missing parts. Only then will Doctor Wogan be allowed to live, and you too."

Doctor Wogan has warned you many times— has even made you swear—to protect the plans with your life. "In the right hands these plans mean peace. In the wrong hands they mean slavery on a scale beyond your wildest imagination." Those had been some of the last words spoken to you by Doctor Wogan before she disappeared.

You stall for time. The man presses you to make a decision. You pretend, talk, beg, ridicule. You are desperate, but you will not yield. His threats don't frighten you; the plans are useless without your vital information—time is on your side, and both of you know it.

The End

Your captor signals to someone down the hill. Minutes later, to your amazement, the woman from the ferry arrives.

"I told you there was danger. I'm surprised you escaped. They meant to kill you," she says.

"It seems I'm no better off now," you answer, hands still stretched skyward.

"You can put your hands down now, but until I'm sure that you mean no harm to Doctor Wogan and her work, you will not be free."

It takes hours of talk to convince her that you are who you say you are.

You look around, noticing that the guard with the gun is relaxed and more interested in his cigar than in you.

"Who are you?" you ask.

"I'm Doctor Wogan's daughter," she replies.

"I never knew Doctor Wogan had a daughter," you say suspiciously.

"Even her close friends know little of the real Doctor Wogan. She was born on this island, and came back here to raise me. You knew her only in your country, after I was old enough to go away to school. Enough talk. Yes or no? Will you help me or not? If you are who you say you are, my mother needs you to help finish the radiation neutralizer."

Turn to page 86.

There is a screeching, tearing sound as time and space collide for a fraction of a moment and then decay. The stone walls and ceiling and floor open up as the molecules lose their hold on one another. When one of the walls falls away, you see Doctor Wogan, a prisoner in the next room. You and Doctor Wogan make your escape; your captors seem overpowered by what has happened and make no move to stop you.

"What now, Doctor Wogan?" you ask.

"Back to London. We'll finish the radiation neutralizer there. It's probably safer, and I'm tired of trying to hide from all these thieves. Everyone wants our plans, but they want them just for themselves. We'll give the plans to the world. That's freedom."

The End

"Let's take cover, Doctor Wogan," you suggest breathlessly. "Maybe they haven't seen us. We can't outrun them." You are already off your horse.

"No! Try to escape," she urges you, and spurs her horse onward. She hands you a duplicate set of the unfinished plans. "Finish these if I'm caught. One of us must make it!" She gallops off.

You watch in horror as she is surrounded by other men who come from the opposite direction.

Now you are alone and in sole possession of the secrets. "I must escape. I must succeed," you say as you scurry into the tangle of brush surrounding the rocky outcroppings of a small hill. "I must escape."

The End

You cast aside the volume. The leather book-mark falls out and the book slides to the far side of the van.

You hold onto the sides of the van for a moment, judging your chances for a successful leap. Then, putting care aside, you leap out, tucking into a ball and rolling when you hit the grassy bank by the side of the road.

Standing up, you watch the van bounce along into the distance. And then you spot it—behind the trees—the roofline of Doctor Wogan's villa.

"Well, I'm out of that one," you say with a sigh of relief. "Now to find Doctor Wogan."

The End

CREDITS

This book is the work of many people. Cathleen Bell and Shannon Gilligan reviewed and edited the original manuscript, bringing it into the Internet age. Shannon Gilligan was executive producer. Laura Arnesen, Melissa Bounty, James Woodard, and Susanne Pingree at Chooseco LLC and Judy Cooper, Kate McQuade, Marlene Stemple, and Ellen Maxwell at Sundance Publishing and Jay Leibold nursed it through various stages of editorial and artistic development. Stacey Hood at Big Eyedea Visual Design in Bigfork, Montana, was responsible for layout and design. Sally Reisner proofread and corrected the final words. Laura Sanderson kept everyone informed and on track. Gordon Troy performed the legal pirouettes that result in proper trademark and copyright protections. Last but not least, Sherry Litwack and Bob Laronga at Sundance acted as godparents. *A very special thanks to Wick Van Heuven.*

Illustrator: Mariano Trod was born in Argentina in 1974. He studied art at the Fine Arts School "Juan Mantovani". Between 1998-2001 he worked as Art Director in the educational cartoon "Astronitos" for Astrokids S.A. Today he is the Art Director for Sismostudio.com

Illustrator: Claudio Griglio was born in Argentina in 1976. He studied with the celebrated Argentinian comic artist Roberto Formento. Claudio was the Director of design at Rafaela City Hall between 2001-2005. Today he is the Coordinator of the illustration department at Sismostudio.com

Illustrator: Andrés Rossi was born in Argentina in 1979. He has a Social Communications degree at the Santiago del Estero Catholic University. He was Junior Designer for Artegraf Design between 1995-1996. He was Junior Designer at the Design Office at Rafaela City Hall between 1996-1999. Between 1999-2002 he worked as Producer on the educational cartoon "Astronitos" for Astrokids S.A. Now he is the CEO of Sismostudio.com

Cover Artist: Jose Luis Marron lives and works in Madrid. He has studied film at universities in Canada and France. Jose worked for several years in the Spanish film and television industry, before turning to design and illustration full-time. He has illustrated seven *Choose Your Own Adventure*® covers.

ABOUT THE AUTHOR

R. A. MONTGOMERY has hiked in the Himalayas, climbed mountains in Europe, scuba-dived in Central America, and worked in Africa. He lives in France in the winter, travels frequently to Asia, and calls Vermont home. Montgomery graduated from Williams College and attended graduate school at Yale University and NYU. His interests include macro-economics, geo-politics, mythology, history, mystery novels, and music. He has two grown sons, a daughter-in-law, and two granddaughters. His wife, Shannon Gilligan, is an author and noted interactive game designer. Montgomery feels that the new generation of people under 15 is the most important asset in our world.

**For games, activities and other fun stuff,
or to write to R. A. Montgomery,
visit us online at CYOA.com**

Look for other titles available now!

CHOOSE YOUR OWN ADVENTURE® 1

THE CLASSIC SERIES IS BACK!
CHOOSE FROM 28 POSSIBLE ENDINGS.

THE ABOMINABLE
SNOWMAN

BY R. A. MONTGOMERY

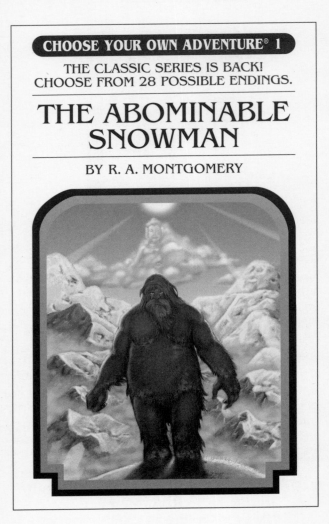

Look for other titles available now!

JOURNEY UNDER THE SEA

BY R. A. MONTGOMERY

Look for other titles available now!

Look for other titles available now!

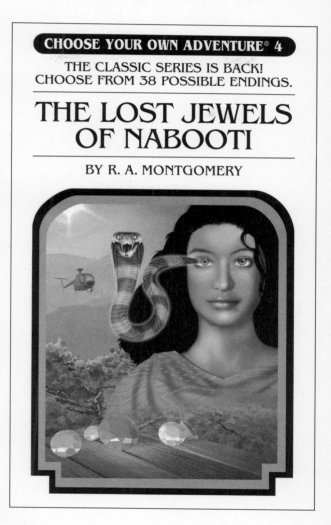

CHOOSE YOUR OWN ADVENTURE® 4

THE CLASSIC SERIES IS BACK!
CHOOSE FROM 38 POSSIBLE ENDINGS.

THE LOST JEWELS OF NABOOTI

BY R. A. MONTGOMERY

Look for other titles available now!

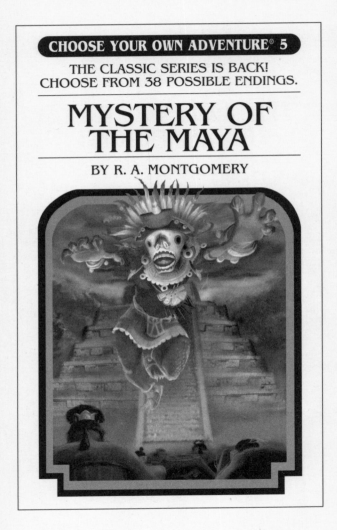

CHOOSE YOUR OWN ADVENTURE® 5

THE CLASSIC SERIES IS BACK!
CHOOSE FROM 38 POSSIBLE ENDINGS.

MYSTERY OF THE MAYA

BY R. A. MONTGOMERY

Look for other titles available now!

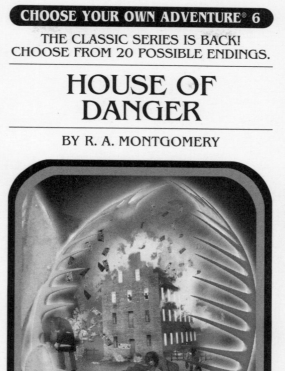

Look for other titles available now!

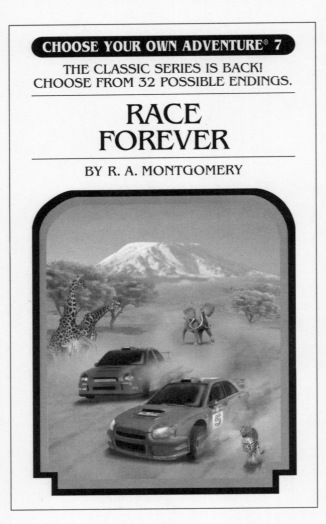

CHOOSE YOUR OWN ADVENTURE® 7

THE CLASSIC SERIES IS BACK!
CHOOSE FROM 32 POSSIBLE ENDINGS.

RACE FOREVER

BY R. A. MONTGOMERY

Look for other titles available now!

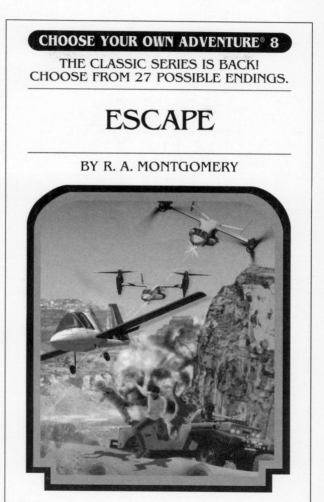

CHOOSE YOUR OWN ADVENTURE® 8

THE CLASSIC SERIES IS BACK!
CHOOSE FROM 27 POSSIBLE ENDINGS.

ESCAPE

BY R. A. MONTGOMERY

Look for other titles coming soon!

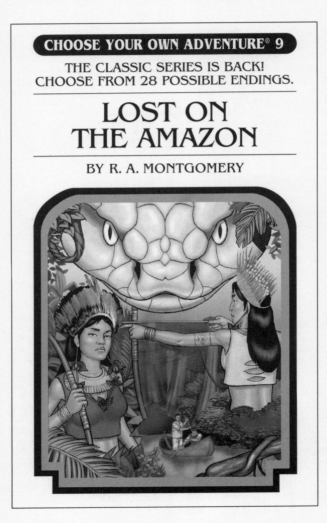

CHOOSE YOUR OWN ADVENTURE® 9

THE CLASSIC SERIES IS BACK!
CHOOSE FROM 28 POSSIBLE ENDINGS.

LOST ON THE AMAZON

BY R. A. MONTGOMERY

CHOOSE YOUR OWN ADVENTURE® 10

THE CLASSIC SERIES IS BACK!
CHOOSE FROM 28 POSSIBLE ENDINGS.

PRISONER OF THE ANT PEOPLE

BY R. A. MONTGOMERY

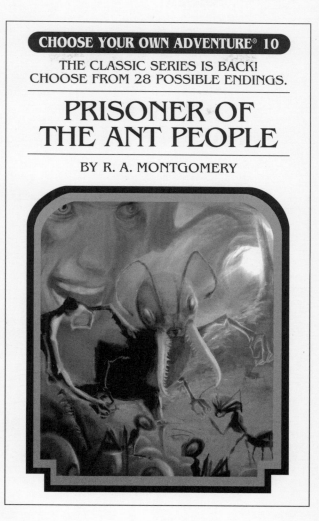

Look for other titles coming soon!

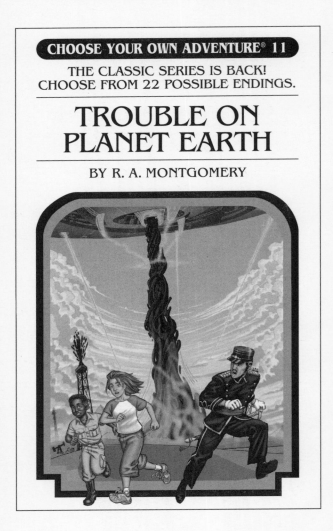

TROUBLE ON PLANET EARTH

BY R. A. MONTGOMERY

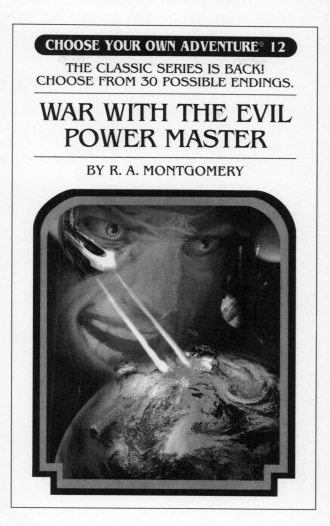

CHOOSE YOUR OWN ADVENTURE® 12

THE CLASSIC SERIES IS BACK!
CHOOSE FROM 30 POSSIBLE ENDINGS.

WAR WITH THE EVIL POWER MASTER

BY R. A. MONTGOMERY

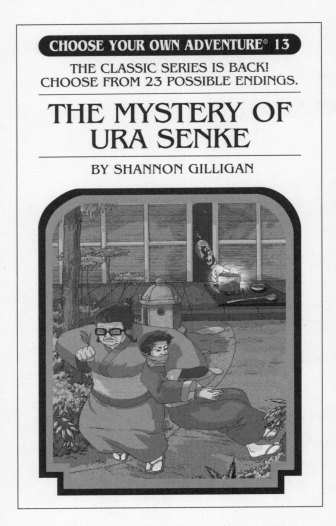

CHOOSE YOUR OWN ADVENTURE® 13

THE CLASSIC SERIES IS BACK!
CHOOSE FROM 23 POSSIBLE ENDINGS.

THE MYSTERY OF URA SENKE

BY SHANNON GILLIGAN

Look for other titles coming soon!

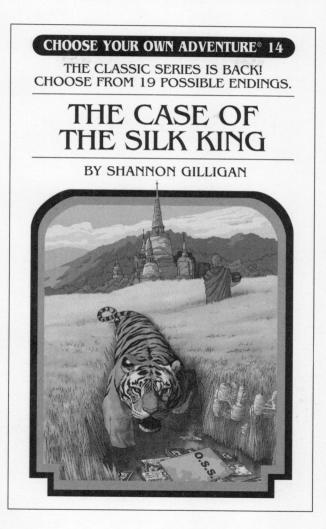

CHOOSE YOUR OWN ADVENTURE® 14

THE CLASSIC SERIES IS BACK!
CHOOSE FROM 19 POSSIBLE ENDINGS.

THE CASE OF
THE SILK KING

BY SHANNON GILLIGAN

O.S.S.

Look for other titles coming soon!

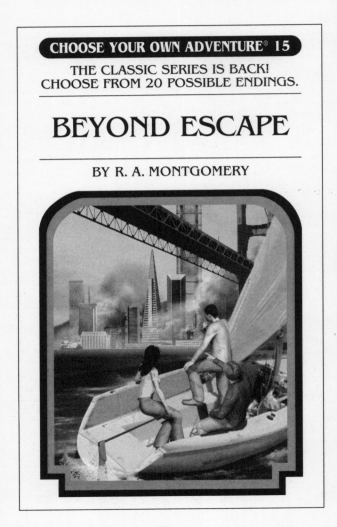

CHOOSE YOUR OWN ADVENTURE® 15

THE CLASSIC SERIES IS BACK!
CHOOSE FROM 20 POSSIBLE ENDINGS.

BEYOND ESCAPE

BY R. A. MONTGOMERY

Look for other titles coming soon!

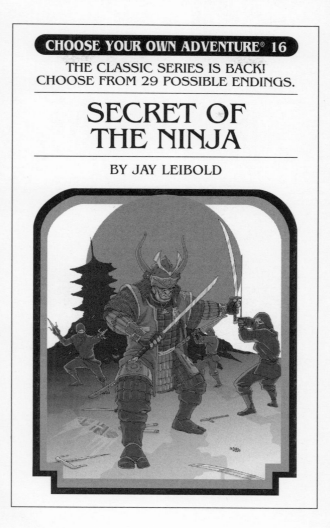

SECRET OF THE NINJA

BY JAY LEIBOLD

Look for other titles coming soon!

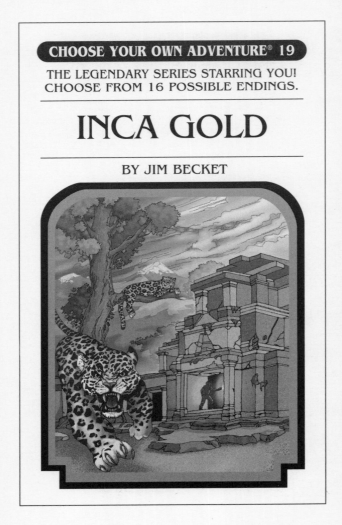

CHOOSE YOUR OWN ADVENTURE® 19

THE LEGENDARY SERIES STARRING YOU!
CHOOSE FROM 16 POSSIBLE ENDINGS.

INCA GOLD

BY JIM BECKET

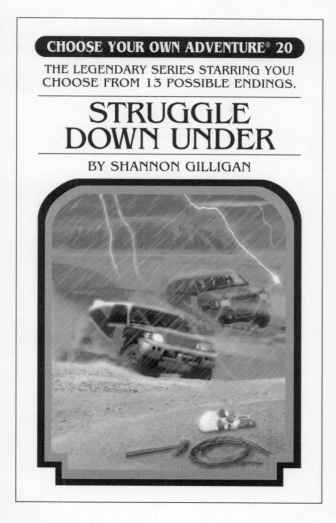

CHOOSE YOUR OWN ADVENTURE® 20

THE LEGENDARY SERIES STARRING YOU!
CHOOSE FROM 13 POSSIBLE ENDINGS.

STRUGGLE DOWN UNDER

BY SHANNON GILLIGAN

Look for other titles coming soon!

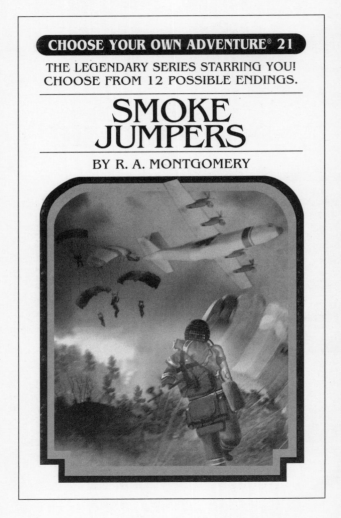

CHOOSE YOUR OWN ADVENTURE® 21

THE LEGENDARY SERIES STARRING YOU!
CHOOSE FROM 12 POSSIBLE ENDINGS.

SMOKE JUMPERS

BY R. A. MONTGOMERY